JAMES
to the
RESCUE
A Book about Friendliness

Janet Noonan and Jacquelyn Calvert
Illustrated by Scott Holladay

Chariot Books™
David C. Cook Publishing Co.

Chariot Books™ is an imprint of David C. Cook Publishing Co.
David C. Cook Publishing Co., Elgin, Illinois 60120
David C. Cook Publishing Co., Weston, Ontario
Nova Distribution Ltd., Newton Abbot, England

JAMES TO THE RESCUE
© 1992 by Janet Noonan and Jacquelyn Calvert for text and Scott Holladay for illustrations

Designed by Terry Julien
First Printing, 1992
Printed in United States of America
96 95 94   5 4 3 2

Library of Congress Cataloging-in-Publication Data
Noonan, Janet, 1915-
James to the rescue / Janet Noonan and Jacquelyn Calvert.
      p.   cm. — (Castle tales)
Summary: Although the Queen seeks to give a pretty ladybug a playmate just like it, it surprises her by befriending three very different insects, bearing out God's commandment that we should all love one another.
ISBN 0-7814-0018-X
[1. Ladybugs—Fiction. 2. Insects—Fiction. 3. Kings, queens, rulers, etc.—Fiction. 4. Christian life—Fiction.]
I. Calvert, Jacquelyn, 1943- II. Title. III. Series: Noonan, Janet, 1915-
Castle tales.
PZ7.N7398Jam   1991
[E]—dc20   91-28574
                                                  CIP
                                                  AC

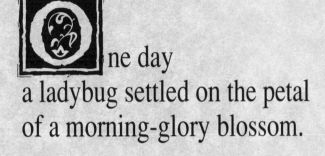

ne day
a ladybug settled on the petal
of a morning-glory blossom.

Flitting from flower to flower, she followed the morning-glory vine up over the wall into the Queen's garden.

There the ladybug saw Her Majesty sitting on a silk cushion. She was sipping tea.

"What a lovely ladybug!" cried the Queen. The ladybug was pleased by the Queen's words and fluttered her wings.

"**I** love her red cloak," said the Queen. "With its shining black dots it looks like a royal robe."

The Queen watched the lovely ladybug while she drank her tea.

Then she remembered, "I have to go to Prince Alfred's coronation today. But my lovely ladybug might get lonesome. Whatever will I do if she flies away home while I am gone? I must see that she has a friend to play with."

"James," she called to her servant, "please search the kingdom for a playmate for my guest. Bring back a friend who is just like her so she will have someone to play with."

James bowed, jumped on his trusty horse, and trotted across the drawbridge into the village.

He came back in a flash.

"Your Majesty, I have found just what you requested." He raised his hat. There on his bare bald head sat a frightened ant.

"Dear me, no!" cried the Queen. "My lovely ladybug would never play with a common working ant. I said a friend who is just like her."

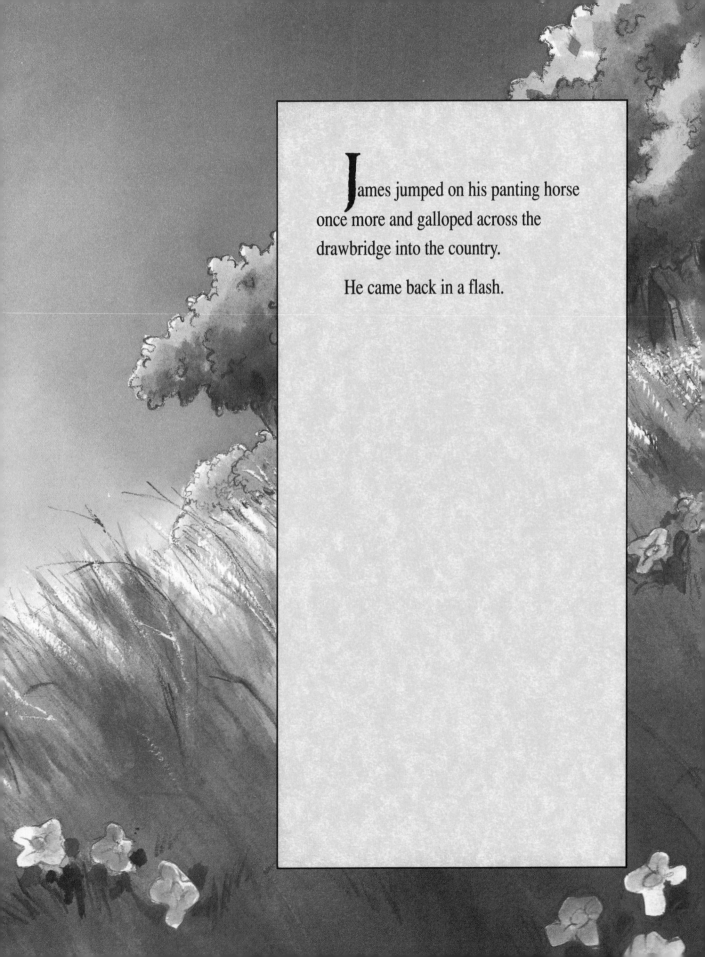

James jumped on his panting horse once more and galloped across the drawbridge into the country.

He came back in a flash.

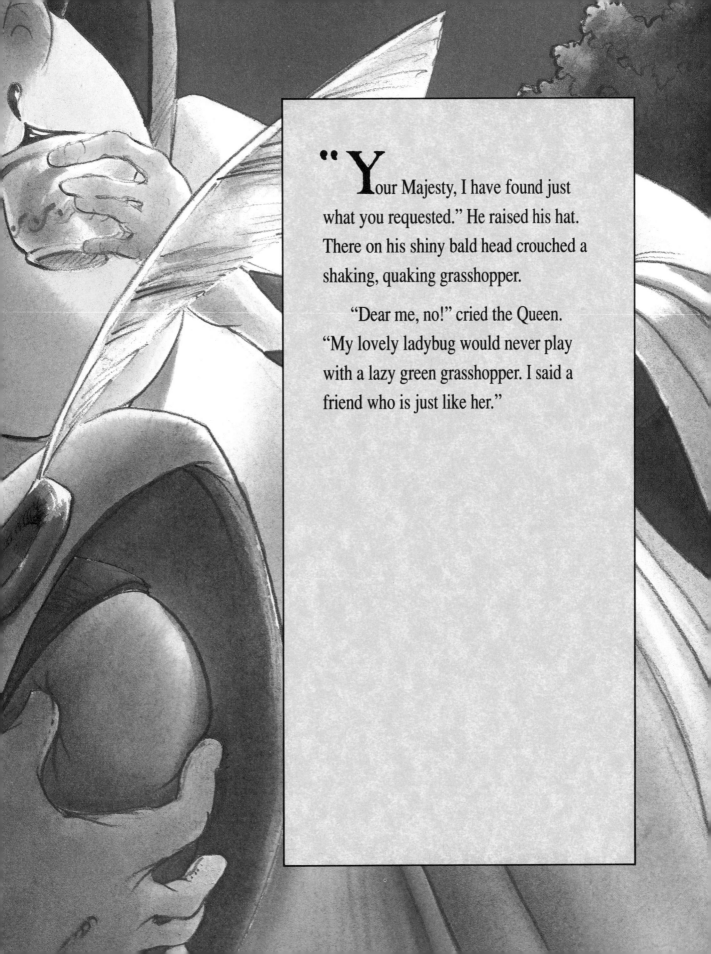

"**Y**our Majesty, I have found just what you requested." He raised his hat. There on his shiny bald head crouched a shaking, quaking grasshopper.

"Dear me, no!" cried the Queen. "My lovely ladybug would never play with a lazy green grasshopper. I said a friend who is just like her."

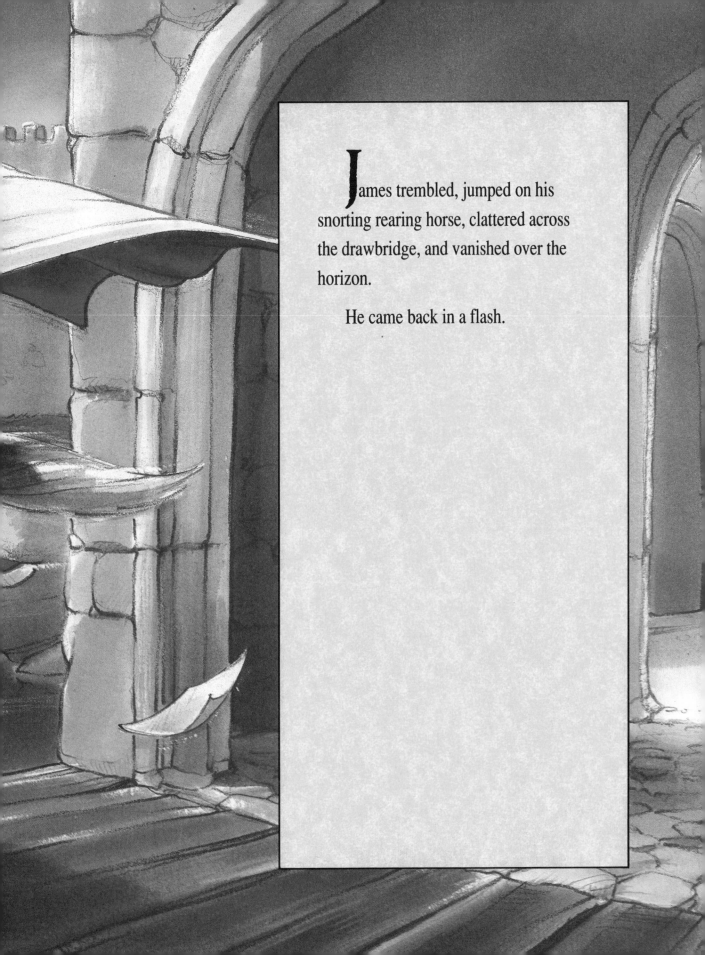

James trembled, jumped on his snorting rearing horse, clattered across the drawbridge, and vanished over the horizon.

He came back in a flash.

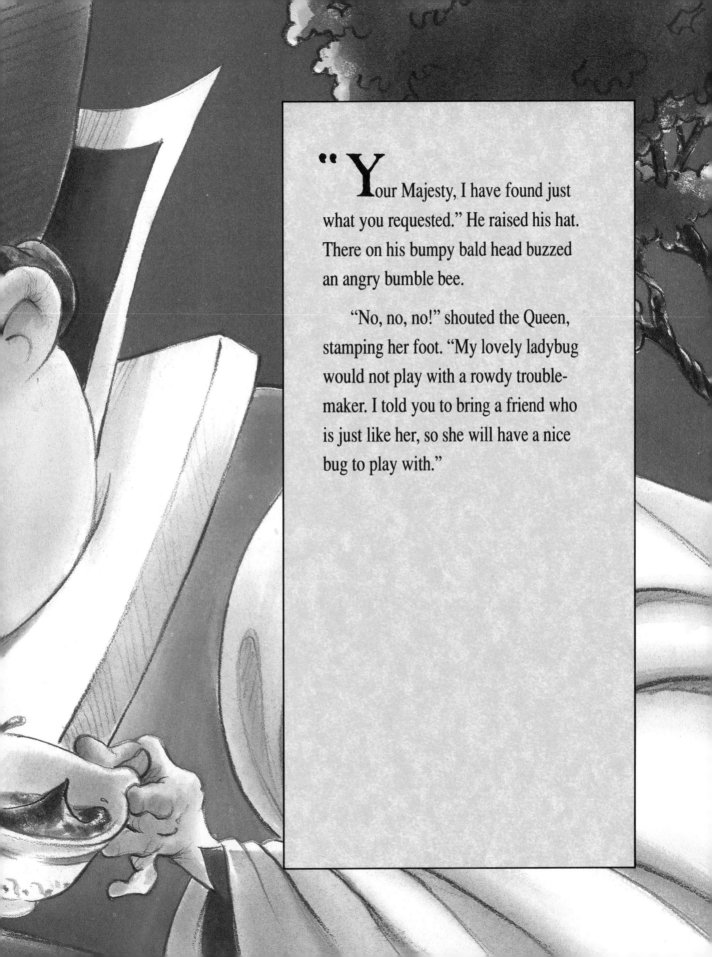

"**Y**our Majesty, I have found just what you requested." He raised his hat. There on his bumpy bald head buzzed an angry bumble bee.

"No, no, no!" shouted the Queen, stamping her foot. "My lovely ladybug would not play with a rowdy trouble-maker. I told you to bring a friend who is just like her, so she will have a nice bug to play with."

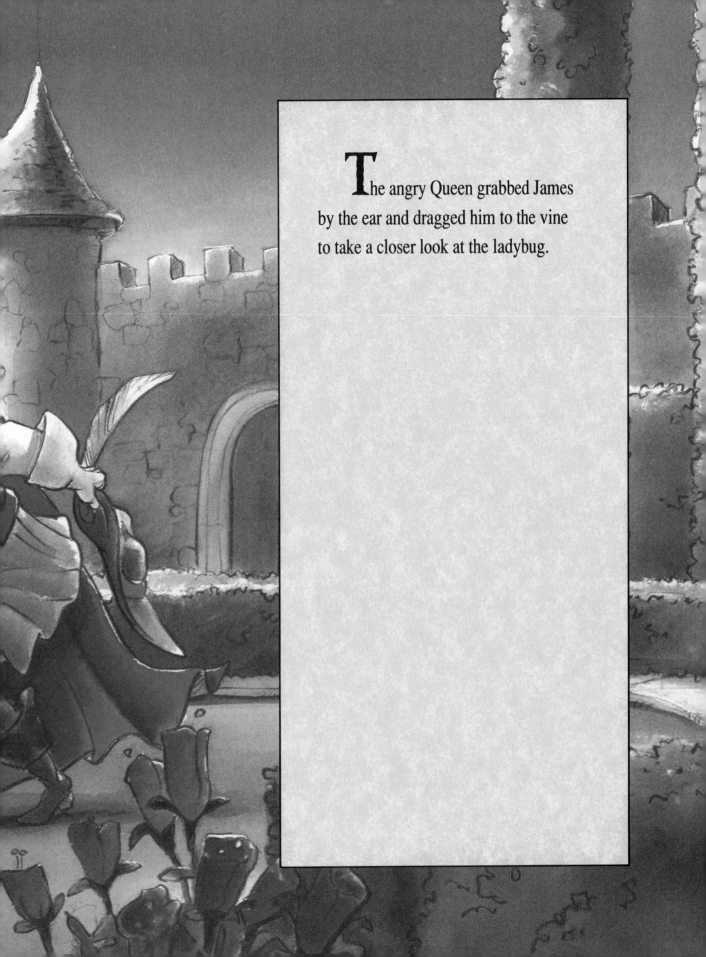

The angry Queen grabbed James by the ear and dragged him to the vine to take a closer look at the ladybug.

Imagine her surprise when, there, on the smiling face of a morning-glory blossom they found a happy foursome drinking tea.

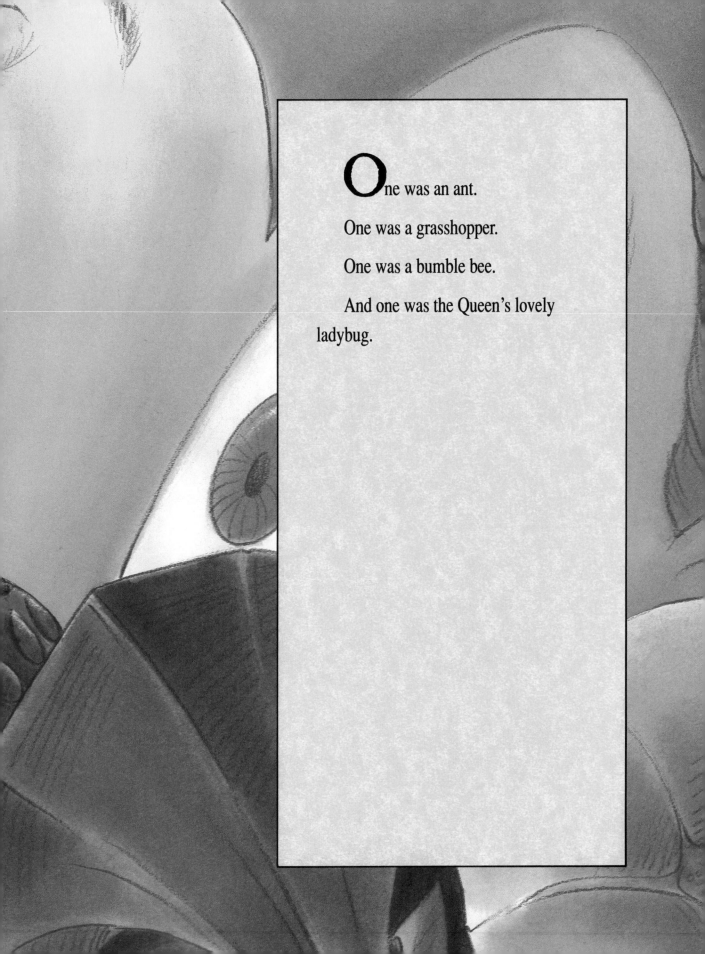

One was an ant.

One was a grasshopper.

One was a bumble bee.

And one was the Queen's lovely ladybug.

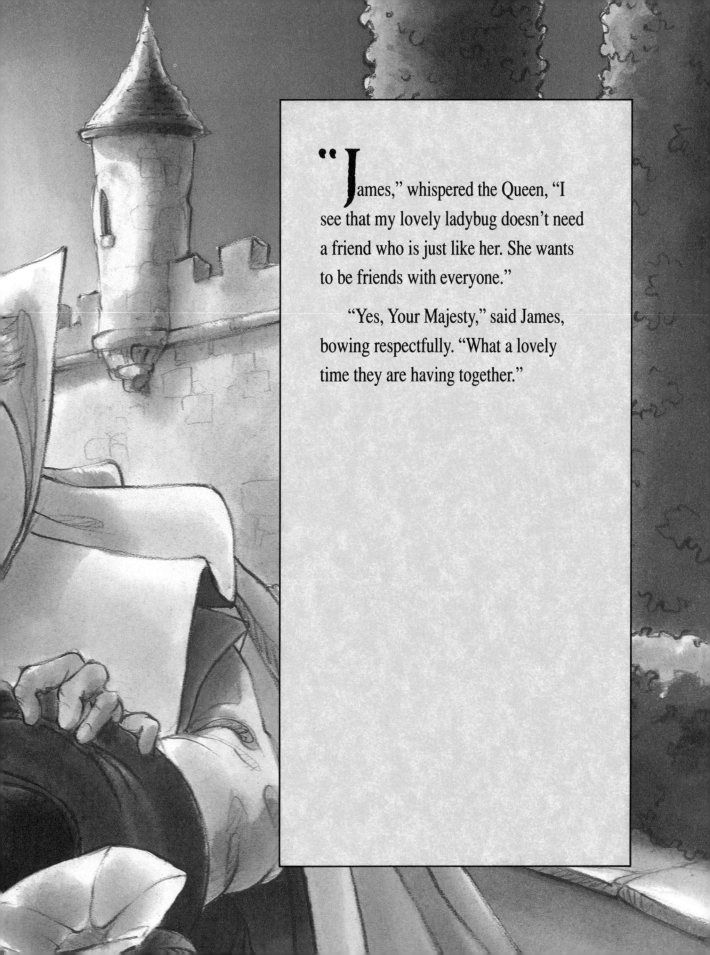

"James," whispered the Queen, "I see that my lovely ladybug doesn't need a friend who is just like her. She wants to be friends with everyone."

"Yes, Your Majesty," said James, bowing respectfully. "What a lovely time they are having together."

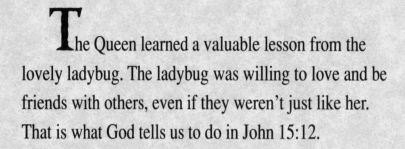

The Queen learned a valuable lesson from the lovely ladybug. The ladybug was willing to love and be friends with others, even if they weren't just like her. That is what God tells us to do in John 15:12.

How can you be a friend to someone today?

This is my commandment,
That ye love one another, as I have loved you.
John 15:12 (KJV)